The worm was a fisherman and he loved to fish. One day, he went fishing with his friends, the frogs. The frog hopped into the water and caught a big fat fish for lunch!

A giraffe always had a long neck and never understood why. One day, her mother told her about the natural benefits of having a long neck. A giraffe can use its neck to reach high branches that short-necked animals could not. It also has better eyesight when looking down on things with its head in the air instead of bending over or laying on the ground to see it up close like most animals do.

The squirrel gets excited when the sun finally shines after such cloudy weather. With a springy step, he goes to one of the trees and jumps on it. There are not enough branches on this tree, so it jumps down again and jumps to the other tree. He doesn't know how high he can go with only these two trees, but there are even more ahead of him! The squirrel is very fond of jumping over the bells

The bird had a moment where she felt like she should sing, but it was hard to find the right song. She wanted to make herself happy and make others around her feel happy too, so she started singing as loudly as possible.

The bear was walking through the forest when he suddenly saw honey dripping from the tree. He came over and licked his tongue a little. Then he noticed that a whole hive of honeycomb was hanging from the branch in front of him. The bear liked honey very much

The hedgehog had thorns. It was a prickly creature and people avoided it for good reason, but the hedgehog didn't care about what other creatures thought. He kept his spines raised just to show that he could, even if it was an invitation to be hurt with no protection against predators.

A worm was looking for a home. He was tired of living in the ground and wanted to find a place that felt right. The little worm travelled far and wide, and found many places along the way. Some were too wet or damp for him, some were too sunny or hot, some had things crawling around in them he didn't like... But then one day he found a spot under an old tree that seemed perfect-- it had soft leaves on the ground. This made him happy and so he decided to live there from now on!

"Wise owl, wise owl, what's the meaning of life?" I ask. The owl looks up from his book and stares at me for a bit before responding with a long silence. "There are many meanings of life." He finally said.

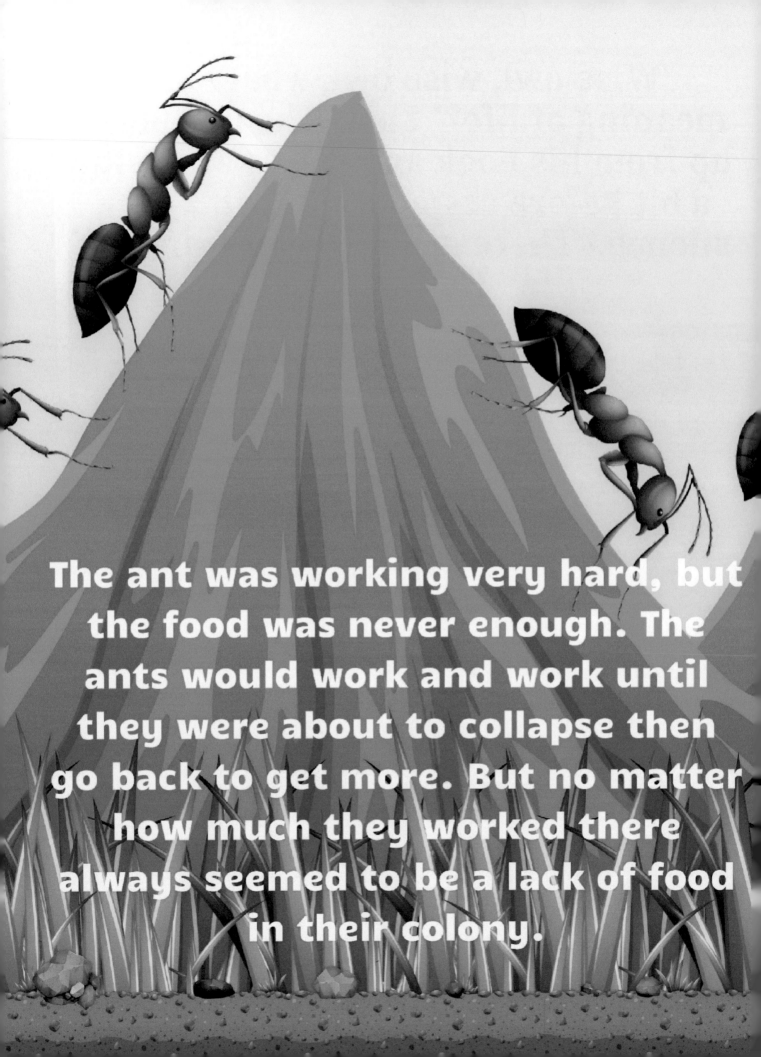

The ant was working very hard, but the food was never enough. The ants would work and work until they were about to collapse then go back to get more. But no matter how much they worked there always seemed to be a lack of food in their colony.

The sun shone brightly on the turtle's shell. He poked his head out of his hole and looked around at the beautiful scene with a content smile. His home was just perfect for him- right in the middle between land and water, he had easy access to both. He could easily swim under or over to get where he needed to be, but if there were any predators near by they would have a harder time getting him!

The sun shone brightly on the turtle's shell. He poked his head out of his hole and looked around at the beautiful scene with a content smile. His home was just perfect for him- right in the middle between land and water, he had easy access to both. He could easily swim under or over to get where he needed to be, but if there were any predators near by they would have a harder time getting him!

The lion was all alone when he met the mane. The mane told him it would make a fine mate. He agreed and they became King of his own Kingdom.

The elephant washes his huge trunk in the clear pond. The water is so refreshing and cool to touch. He then runs up a hill with his head held high because he knows that it's dry on top of the hill, where there are no trees to shade him from the hot sun.

"HEY, LOOK! A ZEBRA!" I SAID TO MY COMPANION. SHE RESPONDED WITH A QUICK GIGGLE AND WE BOTH CONTINUED ON OUR WALK THROUGH THE FOREST. "I WONDER WHERE IT CAME FROM," SHE REMARKED, LOOKING BACK OVER HER SHOULDER.

SUDDENLY WE HEARD A SHRILL NOISE IN THE DISTANCE AND TURNED AROUND JUST AS HE DASHED INTO THE CLEARING BEFORE US AND BEGAN PRANCING ABOUT LIKE AN EXCITED CHILD. I CHUCKLED AT HIS ANTICS WHILE THINKING THAT THOSE STRIPES WOULD MAKE HIM HARD TO FIND IF HE FLED AGAIN FROM WHOEVER WAS MAKING THAT AWFUL SOUND- WHICH WAS QUICKLY GETTING LOUDER BY THE SECOND.

The duck swam and swam in the pond. She was happy because she could swim well.

The bee was buzzing around diligently when it spotted a flower. It buzzed at the flower, and then flew back to its hive where it passed on its knowledge of flowers to other bees about how important they are for their honey production.

The hippo liked to swim in the water. He had a big smile on his face as he drew himself out of the water and onto the shore. His hooves left prints in the sand as he walked off towards some tall grass for some food, hot sun beaming down on his back.

I let the monkey out of his cage and into the pen. I also give him a banana to eat. The monkey, as expected, goes straight for the banana and begins munching away. It's so cute!

The rabbit jumped into the garden and found a carrot. The rabbit ate him, but he soon became very sad because the carrots in his garden are running out. The rabbit is very like of carrots

The kangaroo hops. He jumps from the ground and back down again, his big feet shattering clumps of dirt with every leap. His little joey sits in a pouch on his chest, watching him bounce around like it's some kind of game. The joey tries jumping too, but he just can't keep up with daddy's bouncing pace and sobs louder than ever before. Daddy stops hopping for a minute to look at the joy swinging wildly in its pouch-seat. He says "you want to jump?" which is exactly what the baby wants to do most of all

"The penguin has a suit!" The old man whispered. His friend responded with, "No way! Where did he find it?" "I don't know, but the penguin is wearing it."

The moose had beautiful horns. They looked good when they got up and turned towards her head. She was looking for food in the forest when she saw a red fruit on a tree branch. Only someone can have beautiful horns ...Moose